presented to

_by_

_on_

the
Shoe Box

Written by best-selling author FRANCINE RIVERS

Illustrated by LINDA DOCKEY GRAVES

Tyndale House Publishers, Inc.   Wheaton, Illinois

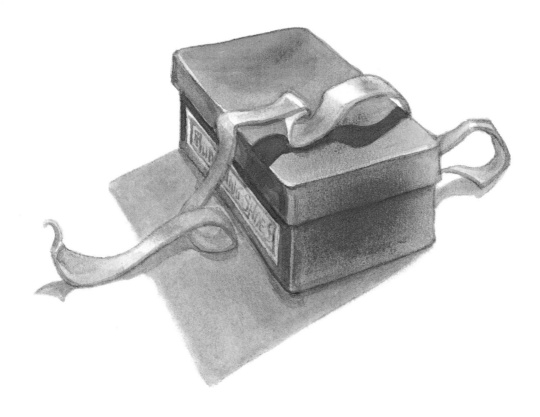

Visit Tyndale's exciting Web site for kids at www.cool2read.com
Also see the Web site for adults at www.tyndale.com

Designed by Julie Chen
Edited by Betty Free Swanberg

This picture book is based on the gift book by the same title, copyright © 1995
by Francine Rivers, published by Tyndale House Publishers under ISBN 0-8423-1901-8.

Library of Congress Cataloging-in-Publication Data
Rivers, Francine, date.
  The shoe box / Francine Rivers.
    p. cm.
  This picture book is based on the gift book of the same title, published by Tyndale House Publishers, © 1995.
  ISBN 1-4143-0568-0
  I. Title.
  PS3568.I83165S46 2005
  813'.54—dc22

                                                                              2004031003

Printed in Singapore
11   10   09   08   07   06   05
7   6   5   4   3   2   1

Timmy O'Neil came to live with Mary and David Holmes on a cloudy day in the middle of September, two weeks after school started. He was a quiet little six-year-old boy with sad eyes. Not very long afterward, they wondered about the box he carried with him all the time. It was an ordinary shoe box with a red lid and the words **Running Shoes** printed on one side.

Timmy carried it everywhere he went. When he did put it down, it was always where he could see it.

"Should we ask him about it?" Mary said to her husband.

"No. He'll talk to us about it when he's ready," David said, but he was as curious as she was.

When Mrs. Iverson, the social worker, came to visit, she said that she was curious about the shoe box too. She told Mary and David that Timmy had the box when the policeman brought him to her office. Timmy's dad had been put in prison. His mom had to work, so Timmy had to be alone all day. A lady in the apartment building where he lived had found out about that and reported it to the police.

"They brought him to me with one small suitcase and that shoe box," Mrs. Iverson said. "I asked him what was inside it, and he said, 'Things.'"

Even the children at Timmy's new school were curious about the box. He would put it on top of his desk while he did his work.

His first grade teacher, Mrs. King, asked, "What do you have there, Timmy?"

"My box," he said.

"What's in your box?"

"Things," he said and went on with his arithmetic.

Mrs. King didn't want to keep asking about the box. She liked Timmy, and she didn't want to pry. She told Mary and David that Timmy was a good student. He always tried to do his best. Mrs. King wrote a note to him on one of his math papers. "Other students will learn by your example," the note said. She drew a big smiley face on his paper and gave him a pretty, sparkly star sticker.

Mary Holmes learned that Timmy liked chocolate chip cookies, so she kept the cookie jar full. Timmy would come home from school on the yellow bus and sit at the kitchen table after putting the box under his chair. Mary always sat with him and asked him about his day while he had milk and cookies.

Every evening when he came home from work, David played catch with Timmy in the backyard. Timmy always brought the box outside with him and set it on the lawn chair where he could see it.

Timmy even took the shoe box with him to Sunday school. And when he went to bed at night, the shoe box sat on the nightstand beside his bed.

Timmy got letters from his mother twice a week. Once she sent him ten dollars and a short note from his father. Timmy cried when Mary read it to him because his father said how much he missed Timmy and how sorry he was about the wrong things he had done. Mary held Timmy on her lap in the rocking chair for a long time.

One evening David and Mary took Timmy to see a movie about a lion. They both noticed Timmy's expression of wonder and delight.

When Timmy got off the school bus the next day, he was surprised to find David waiting for him. "Hi, Champ," David said. "I thought I'd come home early and share your special day." He ruffled Timmy's hair and walked with him to the house.

When they came in the kitchen door, Mary leaned down and kissed Timmy on the cheek. "Happy birthday, Timmy."

The boy's eyes widened in surprise as he saw a big box on the kitchen table. It was wrapped in pretty paper and tied up with bright-colored ribbons.

Timmy put his old shoe box on the table and opened the bigger box with the pretty paper. In it he found a lion just like the one in the movie. Hugging it, he laughed.

Mary turned away so Timmy wouldn't see the tears in her eyes. David put his arm around her. It was the first time they had seen Timmy smile or laugh about anything. And it made them very happy.

When Mary put the birthday cake on the table and lit the candles, David took her hand and then Timmy's and said a prayer of blessing and thanksgiving. "Go ahead, Timmy. Make a wish and blow out the candles." Timmy didn't have to think very long about what he wished, and when he blew, not a candle was left burning.

Timmy's mother came to visit every other week. She and Timmy sat together in the living room. She asked him about school, and she asked if he was happy with David and Mary Holmes. He said he was, but he still missed her. She held him and stroked his hair back from his face. She told him she missed him, too, but it was more important that he have a safe place to grow up. "These are nice people, Timmy."

Each time before she left, she always told him to be good. She picked him up and held him tightly for a long time before she kissed him and put him down again. Timmy was always sad and quiet when she left.

In the fall, Mary's mother and father came for Thanksgiving. Timmy liked them. Mary's mother played Monopoly with him, and her father told him funny fishing stories.

Friends came to join them for dinner, and the house was full of happy people. Timmy had never seen so much food on one table. He tried everything. When dinner was over, David gave him the wishbone. He told Timmy to let it dry and then they'd pull on it to see who would get to make a wish.

December came and brought with it colder weather. Mary and David bought Timmy a heavy snow parka and gloves. His mother gave him a new backpack, and he put his shoe box in it. He carried it to school each day, and in the afternoon he'd hang the backpack on the closet door, where he could see it while he was doing his homework or when he went to bed at night.

It seemed everybody in the small town where Mary and David Holmes and Timmy lived knew about the shoe box. But only Timmy knew what was inside it.

Sometimes children on the bus would ask him what he had in the box, but he'd say, "Just things."

"What kind of things?"

He would shrug, but he would never say.

The church where Mary and David Holmes took Timmy had a Christmas program each year. Everyone dressed in costumes. This year part of the program was to include acting out the Nativity while the choir sang.

"We need lots of children for the parts," Chuck, the program director, said. "The choir will sing about the angels who spoke to the shepherds in the fields. And there's a song about the wise men who came from faraway lands to see Jesus. And, of course, we need a girl to play Mary and a boy to play Joseph."

"What about Jesus?" Timmy said.

"Latasha has a baby brother," one of the girls said. "She could be Mary, and her baby brother can be Jesus."

"That's a great idea," Chuck said.

Chuck noticed the look on Timmy's face when all the parts were filled. He said to Timmy, "We could use another shepherd."

"I'd like to be a wise man."

There were already three wise men, but Chuck thought about it and nodded his head. "You know, the Bible doesn't say how many wise men came to see Jesus. There might have been four. There might have been more than that. I'll ask the lady making costumes if she can make one more for you."

The lady was very happy to make a costume for Timmy. She spent extra time on it because she wanted it to be very special. She made a long blue robe that went to his ankles. She made a sash of many colors and a long coat of a beautiful brocade with purple and gold. Then she made a turban for his crown and put a big rhinestone on the front and some colored feathers in the top.

When the night came for the program, everyone was so excited that no one noticed Timmy holding his old shoe box instead of the fancy jewelry box he was supposed to carry.

One by one the wise men laid down their gifts for Jesus, but everyone sitting in the audience in the big church social hall was looking at Timmy. Timmy's mother had come to see him in the program. Mrs. Iverson, the social worker, had come as well. So had Mrs. King, his schoolteacher.

They all held their breath when it was Timmy's turn to lay down his offering. He looked like a real king in his royal clothes. The lights were on him, and the sparkles on his coat made him shine. With both hands he carried the old, worn shoe box with the red lid and the words **Running Shoes** printed on the side, presenting it with solemn respect to little Jesus.

Timmy stood up. He turned and smiled at his mother and at Mary and David, Mrs. Iverson, and Mrs. King. Then he took his place among the other wise men.

Timmy sang with the choir. And he didn't worry about the precious shoe box. In fact, he didn't look at it once. His family and friends had never seen him look so happy.

When the program was over, Timmy's mother took his hand and went with him for punch and Christmas cookies. Mary and David went with them. So did Mrs. Iverson and Mrs. King. They all said how proud they were of him.

When it came time to go, Timmy's mother asked him if he wanted to get his shoe box.

"Oh no," Timmy said. "I gave it to Jesus."

In heaven an angel, kneeling before Jesus, said, "Here it is, my Lord."
The angel held out the old shoe box with the words **Running Shoes** printed on it.

Jesus took it and set it on his lap. He looked out at the thousands of
angels, who were curious about what was inside. Only Jesus and Timmy
knew.

An angel asked, "What's in that box, Lord? What has the child given
you?"

"Just things," Jesus said, smiling. He had watched Timmy even before he
was born. He had counted every hair on his head and knew all that was in
his heart. And he had waited for the day when the child would come to him
with all he had to offer.

Jesus took the top off the shoe box, and the angels leaned forward as he took out one item at a time and laid it tenderly upon his lap.

And what they saw were just things:

The worn and faded silk edge of his baby blanket
A wedding picture of his mother and father
His mother's letters
Ten dollars
His father's note of love and apology
A math paper with a smiley face and a note from his teacher
A pretty star sticker

A movie ticket stub
Used birthday candles
A bright curled ribbon
The big side of a broken turkey wishbone

There were things in the box you couldn't see too. Hopes, dreams, prayers, and many worries and fears. All of them were in the box Timmy gave to Jesus.

With tender care, Jesus put everything back in the shoe box. He looked at the angels and said, "Timmy has given the most precious gift of all: the faith of a child."

After that, angels never left Timmy's side.

They were with him when Mary and David invited Timmy's mother to come and live with them. They were with him when Mary and David had a baby of their own. The angels were with him when his father got out of prison in time for his high school graduation. They surrounded Timmy as he grew up, married, and had children of his own.

In fact, angels surrounded him and protected him all the days of his life. Finally, the time came for them to go with him to heaven. He went straight into the waiting arms of Jesus, who loved him very much.

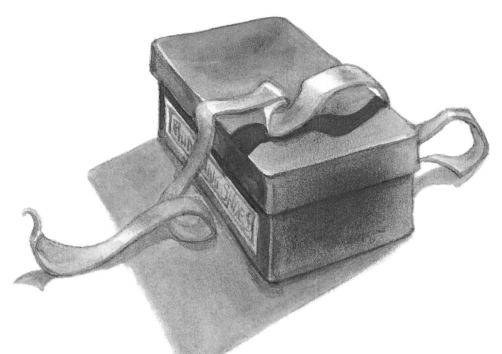

How This Story Came to Be

When I first became a Christian, one of the hardest things for me to do was give my burdens to the Lord. I would worry over all kinds of things.

I remember a friend talking about putting prayers in a lunch bag, and that got me thinking. One of the many jobs I had held was that of a secretary, and I remembered the "in" and "out" boxes. From that memory came the idea of a "God box." I took an ordinary cardboard container with a lid and covered it with beautiful wrapping paper. Then I cut a slot in the top. Whenever something was bothering me greatly and I couldn't let it go, I would write out a prayer about it. Then I would tuck the written prayer into the God box. Sometimes my husband and my children would write prayers and tuck them into the box as well. It was amazing to me how this physical exercise helped me give up worries and burdens to the Lord.

Every few months I would open the box and read the prayers. What I found was a source of great joy and comfort, for many of the prayers were answered, often in completely unexpected ways.

My God box gave me the idea for "The Shoe Box." While I put worries and burdens in my box, I wanted Timmy to put blessings and praises in his box as well. It reminded me that there are all kinds of prayers—worship and praise as well as cries for help. Scripture says the prayers of believers are the sweet scent of incense to the Lord.

Francine Rivers